# Pete

*A short comedy by*

Scott Frank

*Pete* by Scott Frank



2nd Edition
**ISBN 978-0-557-02654-8**

Printed in the US by Lulu Publishing

## Character List

Peter Pan

Wendy

Captain Hook

The Darling Brothers

Smee

Lost Boy 1

Lost Boy 2

Tinkerbella

Peter's Mom

Peter's Dad

# "Pete"
By Scott Frank

## **Scene 1**

(Peter is in Wendy's room looking for his shadow)

Peter. Shadow?

Peter. Shadow, where are you?

Peter. Oh shadow?

Peter. There you are.

Wendy. Who are you and what are you doing in my house? Stranger danger!!

Peter. Oh, hey! I'm Peter Pan

Wendy. You're Peter Pan? Oh, I've heard so much about you. Well, my name is Wendy

Peter. Isn't that a girl's name

Wendy. NO! It's a man's name.

Peter. What ever you say Cindy?

Wendy. It's Wendy.

Peter. Wendy, it's nice to meet you

Wendy. Oh, who's that?

Peter. That's my fairy Tinkerbella

Tinkerbella. Hey Baby! Like what you see?

Wendy. Tinker-what?

Tinkerbella. It's Tinkerbella!

Wendy. Oh, Peter I'd like you to meet my brothers John and Michael.

Darling Brothers. Hi! We're conjoined twins!

Peter: Umm…nice to meet you guys.

Wendy. Peter; is that your shadow running around my room?

Peter. Aw, he got away again. You know, I have no idea what has gotten in to him. Lately, he's been trying to escape me a lot. Come back shadow!

(Peter chases his shadow. He tries to put the shadow back on.)

Wendy. Why, that's not how you put a shadow on. You ought to sew it on like this.

(Wendy sews Peter's shadow back on.)

Peter. Thanks, Wendy. Well, I have to go now. Come on Tinkerbella!

Tinkerbella. Boy, don't tell me what to do!

Wendy. Wait where are you going?

Peter. Why, to Neverland of course.

Wendy. What is that?

Peter. You mean you don't know what Neverland is? Why, Neverland is the most wonderful place ever. I created it so that you could do anything your heart desires and best of all there are no parents to ruin the fun! Come on! I'll show you.

Wendy. That sounds terrific!

Peter. Oh, and bring your brothers too I'm sure they'll

enjoy Neverland as much as you will.

Wendy. But how do we even get to Neverland?

Peter. Fly of course!!!

Wendy. Fly? But we can't fly!

Peter. Sure you can…with my pixie potion.

Wendy. Pixie potion?

Peter. Yeah! All you need is a little pixie dust…

Tinkerbella. What? No!

(Peter grabs Tinkerbella and proceeds to shake her)

Tinkerbella. Oh yeah! Shake me! Shake me but don't break me!

Peter. And happy thoughts…anything is possible. Here, I'll show you.

(Peter proceeds to sing a little song)

Peter. Pixie Potion,

Help us to fly,

Because there's nothing to make us high,

Please give us the gift of flight,

Pixie Potion help us to fly.

Wendy. Peter, I'm scared. I don't know about leaving my parents without telling them.

Peter. It's alright…just take my hand, and close your eyes, everything's going to be all right.

Peter. Come on guys, it's off to Neverland!

Tinkerbella. Dang! Don't you know how to wait for a lady?

## Scene 2

(Captain Hook is looking for Smee in his cabin on his ship.)

Captain Hook. Smee!!!

Captain Hook. Smee!! Where are you?

Smee. Yes Captain Hook?

Captain Hook. Why are you that close to me...take a step back...another one...that's good...

Captain Hook. Smee, I am not paying you lollygag around the deck. I am paying you to count my money--like this—ONE, one dollar bill; TWO, one dollar bill. So forth and so on.

Captain Hook. Smee I can feel it...these seas are mine for the taking!

Smee. Don't you mean ours?

Captain Hook. Well, of course you'll receive some land, Smee. I mean who else will keep it clean?

Smee. Yes sir.

Captain Hook. But there is one person in the way of my greatness.

Smee. Who sir?

Captain Hook. (gags) I will barf if I say his name. I really will.

Smee. Oh! Peter Pan!

(Captain Hook slaps Smee.)

Captain Hook. Don't say that name around me like that!

Smee. Peter Pan!

(Captain Hook slaps Smee again.)

Captain Hook. Stop laughing!

(Captain Hook slaps Smee yet another time.)

Smee. Peter Pan, Peter Pan, Peter Pan.

Captain Hook. STOP IT!!!!

Captain Hook. Now look at what you've gone and made me do. You made me hit you. I didn't want to hurt you but I had to keep my Hook strong

Captain Hook. Now back to Peter Pan, the boy wonder, in the green tights…he must be finished!

Smee. Why do you hate him so much Captain Hook?

Captain Hook. Why do I hate him so much? Why? I'll tell you why!

(Captain Hook has a flash back)

Captain Hook. Hey there little boy, what's you name?

Peter. I'm Peter Pan!

Captain Hook. Such a beautiful name…oh, you want a lollipop, I know you want it.

Peter. No!

(Peter cuts off Hooks hand)

Captain Hook. Now look what you've gone and done. You got blood all over my shirt.

(Flashback ends)

Captain Hook. And that's why I've dedicated my life to the downfall of that boy. He must be taken care of.

Smee. Like…

(Smee cuts his throat.)

Captain Hook. No, I was thinking along the lines of …

(Captain Hook puts his Hook in his mouth to resemble a fish caught in a Hook)

Smee. Oh my! But how will we even find Peter Pan? We don't know where his hideout is?

Captain Hook. That's a good question…why go to the boy, when the boy can come to us. All we need to do is capture Tinkerbella and he'll come in no time to rescue her. Then when he's most vulnerable, we'll Hook him (laughs) that's funny because I got the hook. And… (looks at Smee) Damn you're ugly.

## **Scene 3**

(Peter and the Darlings are flying in the sky over Neverland)

Wendy. Oh Peter, I haven't had this much fun in a long time!

Peter. Look! We're finally here in Neverland.

Wendy. Why it's beautiful!

Pirates. Fire!

Wendy. Oh no! That boat is shooting at us!

Peter. It's Hook's henchmen! Tinkerbella! Quick! Get Wendy and her brothers out of here. I'll distract the boat

Tinkerbella. Ok.

Wendy. Wait! Tinkerbella you're going to fast!

Tinkerbella. He-he-he…

Wendy. Tinkerbella where are you?

(Tinkerbella flies away. Wendy and his brothers are left to be barricaded by canons. One of those canons hits Wendy.)

Wendy. Where am I?

(Peter finds Wendy and flies down to her.)

Peter. Well, you were in Neverland for two seconds, but then you got blasted with a cannon. So now your dead and waiting for the gates of hell to open so you can burn for eternity.

Wendy. What?

Peter. No I'm just joking with you. You're still alive. Come on Wendy, there's two people I'd like you to meet.

(Lost boys appear and start to chant.)

Lost Boy 1&2. Oo! Oo! Aw! Aw!

Lost Boy 1. Hey!

Peter. Wendy, these are the Lost boys.

Lost Boy 1. Get it right Peter, we are not the *Lost Boys*, we are lost, boy!

Lost Boy 2. Ooh Wendy, do you like our new war outfits? It's made out of Chewbacca fur. I'm just kidding, it's something else; we just like the fur.

Lost Boy 2. Oh my, what is that Peter?

Peter. Oh! This is Shirley.

Wendy. It's Wendy.

Peter. Wendy…Okay.

Lost Boy 1. What's a Wendy?

Lost Boy 2. It looks a hot mess to me.

Lost Boy 1. Girl, I like your fur!

Lost Boy 2. This is not fur, this is chinchilla.

Lost Boy 2. Well, mine is leopard.

Lost Boy 1. Girl say that again!

Lost Boy 2. Leopard.

Lost Boy 1. Ooh one more time!

Lost Boy 2. Leopard.

Lost Boy 1. Ooh, it gives me chills.

Lost Boy 2. Girl, they also have jaguar, cheetah, and tiger.

Wendy. They look nice ladies.

Lost Boy 1&2. LADIES?!

Lost Boy 1. At least you look better than you! What are you doing here anyways? You don't belong here!

Lost Boy 2. So why don't you go home cause nobody wants you see you're stupid face.

Wendy. ...Fine....

(Wendy flies off)

## **Scene 4**

(Wendy is alone in the woods.)

(Smee comes up from behind and captures her.)

Smee. Hello Wendy, I believe Captain Hook would like to have a word with you.

(Smee beings Tinkerbella back to Captain Hook's ship.)

Smee. Captain Hook, look!

Captain Hook. What is it Smee. Smee where are you?

Smee. I'm right here Captain Hook…

Captain Hook. Take a step back Smee…another one...so what do you want?

Smee. Look! I have Peter Pan's friend!

Captain Hook. Oh wow!

( Wendy is tied up. She is angry at them.)

Captain Hook. Angry little fellow isn't she. Look Wendy, are you going to tell me where Peter Pan is?

Smee. Or are we going to have to force it out of you.

Wendy. I'm not telling you anything!

Captain Hook. Fine! Then Peter will just find your lifeless body while I get him myself.

**Scene 5**

Lost Boy 1. Peter! Peter!

Peter. What! What!

Lost Boy 1. So, Peter, we found this letter outside and we're afraid it's bad new…we didn't know how to tell you. So we decided to but it in song. Come on girl.

Lost Boy 1 & 2.

Dear Peter Pan,
Let me tell you my great plan
I got someone dear to you
So here's a clue I'll give to you
In the sea is where you'll look
For two black sails with a Hook
Love Captain Hook.

Lost Boy 2 Yay! Good job girl.

Peter Pan. Wendy! Oh no we have to save her!

Lost Boy 1. Oh good we get to use our new war outfits.

Peter. I wonder who captured her….

Lost Boy 1. Hook!

Peter. No.

Lost Boy 1. Yes.

Peter. No.

Lost Boy 1. Yes

Peter. Hook?

Lost Boy 1. Hook!

Peter. You mean with the…

Lost Boy 1. Hook!

Peter. Come on every one suit up and prepare for glory! For Neverland!

Lost Boy 1. For Neverland!

Lost Boy 2. For Narnia! I mean Neverland!

(Peter and the Lost boys fly off to Captain Hook's ship.)

Smee. Captain Hook! Captain Hook!

Captain Hook. What! What!

Smee. We're under attack by Peter Pan!

Captain Hook. Peter Pan?

Smee. Peter Pan!

Captain Hook. No.

Smee. Yes.

Captain Hook. No.

Smee. Yes.

Captain Hook. Peter Pan?

Smee. Peter Pan!

Captain Hook. You mean the little boy that wears green tights.

Smee. Yes!

Captain Hook. Arg! Ready the cannons! Let the war begin!

(Peter goes to Captain Hook's ship)

Peter. Hook! Where's Wendy?!

Hook. I don't know.

(Peter pulls sword out on Hook)

Peter. Tell me, or I'll…

Hook. Humph…I've been waiting for this moment for way too long. Bring it on.

(Everyone start to battle one another. Hook dies in the process.)

Peter. He's dead…he's finally dead! We can all live in peace now.

Peter. Oh no! I forgot about Wendy.

(Peter goes to free Wendy.)

Peter. So now that everyone is safe, we should go back to my hideout and plan our next adventure.

Wendy. Um Peter, I think me and my brothers had enough adventures for one day. Can we go home now?

Peter. What! Why? Neverland is great! Why would you want to go home? Here, you never have to worry, never have to grow up. Don't you like it here Wendy?

Wendy. Yes! Of course I like it here, but our parents will miss us and I miss them too

Peter. What about me? I'll miss you. You're the only friend I've got. You don't need them. We could be your family and Neverland could be your home! This place has everything you need.

Darling Brothers. So, does that mean that we're all brothers?

Lost Boys. Umm Peter, I think you might want to reconsider what you just said.

Wendy. I know but my parents…

Peter. Parents? Why do you even bother? All this time you've been here, have you seen them looking for you? Don't you see that they don't really care about you? Your parents are no different than mine. They only worry about themselves and their busy adult lives. They don't have time for kids.

Wendy. You don't get it do you? This can never be my home.

Peter. Why not?!

Wendy. It's because this place isn't real.

Peter. What are you talking about? Of course it's real.

Wendy. No Peter, Neverland is all in your head. It's all imaginary. I think you've created this place to escape your parents.

(Peter has a flashback. He flies to the window that use to belong to his home and starts knocking.)

Peter. Mom! Dad! I'm home! I'm back from Neverland!!

(Peter's dad is rocking in a chair. The baby in his arms cries.)

Peter's Mom. Honey, what's all that knocking?

(Peter's dad looks back towards the window and sees Peter. He tries to remember Peter but fails to recall. He thinks it is only a figment of his imagination.)

Peter's Dad. Oh, it's nothing, nothing.

(Peter's dad closes the shade as he turns back around.)

Peter. Dad! Don't you remember me? It's me! Pete…

(Peter tries to peek through a crack and watches emotionally. Flashback ends.)

Peter. That's right. I created this place, not to escape my parents but because my parents abandoned me. I went back and knocked on that door every single night. But I never got a reply. If they cared they would've answered for their son. Parents forget about you. They get caught up with their own lives and don't even notice that their own son is gone.

Wendy. Peter…

Peter. No!

Wendy. But not all parents are like that.

Peter. Yes they are! Parents only want you because they like the ideal of a family, but once they realize what it really takes to raise a child, they push you away!

Wendy. Come on Peter, that's not true. My parents are not like that?

Peter. Yes they are. You just haven't noticed it yet.

Peter. Your parents don't love you like my parents didn't love me.

Wendy. Peter, I'm sorry that your parents don't want you. They made a big mistake in doing so, but you can't blame every parent for the way your mom and dad act. You know, if you want, I'm sure my parents can take you in. They'll love you as much as they love me.

Peter. That's impossible. If my own parents didn't want me why would yours?

Wendy. Well just like you said, "With a little pixie dust and happy thoughts anything is possible".

Peter. I don't want to hear it. They're all the same. They're all cruel. Now if you want me to take you home then fine but don't tell me that I didn't warn you.

(Peter takes Wendy home. Wendy is reunited with his parents.)

Peter. You don't have to go.

Wendy. I'm sorry Peter. You know, it's not too late to change your mind. Think about it, Peter.

(Wendy enters her house though the window. Her parents are there waiting for her. They rejoice.)

Wendy. Mom! Dad! I missed you so much! I'll never leave you guys again. Mom, Dad, there's someone I'd like you to meet.

(Peter steps out from the shadows)

Peter. Hi…I'm Pete.

*Pete* by Scott Frank

# End.

*Pete* by Scott Frank

*Pete* by Scott Frank

*Pete* by Scott Frank

www.ingramcontent.com/pod-product-compliance
Ingram Content Group UK Ltd.
Pitfield, Milton Keynes, MK11 3LW, UK
UKHW020228250726
13967UKWH00001B/247